Published by:

The Man with More Lives Than a Cat ™

www.themanwithmorelivesthanacat.com

ISBN: 979-8-9850415-2-1

Cover Design & Interior Layout:

Bryan K. Reed, www.bryankreed.com

Printed in the United States

David Goliath and the Arctic Miracle.
Is there Life After Death?

Through the darkness of my own death, and the light of rebirth, can I discover mystical powers to see my future that will not only alter my own destiny but also that of the entire world?

This is not a story - it is a journey!

Along my life's path of more than 85 years I have experienced over 24 life-threatening events that I desperately try to forget, but then realize they are agonizing tests of my will to live and go on. This is its message to live each day of loneliness with hope for a better tomorrow, have faith in yourself and a greater power, believe in all those you care for and those who care for you.

From the team of
W D Evans and H M Logue.
A short story based upon the True-Life adventure novel.

"Searching For The Good War".
by W D Evans.
The Man With More Lives Than a Cat
"It's never too late to make your Dreams come true"

Contents

Dedication

To Annie, my true Angel, my Inspiration to jump over impossible fences no matter how tall, my Unconditional Love for over 60 years, and still counting.

To Doctor Russell Varian, whose marvelous invention saved me from freezing to death in the Arctic.

To my deserting Father who taught me to be self-reliant and that I must create whatever I needed in life to survive.

To my Mother who always told me I was just a dreamer. She was absolutely right.

To my creative book designer who has more than tolerated my many updates to make it "Just Right."

To all those in my family who always helped me believe that my impossible dreams could come true.

To my Grandson, Benjamin Smitty, who tirelessly listened to my many adventures and told me I had lived more lives than a cat. Thus, to his credit, I became "The Man with More Lives Than a Cat."

Warning

This is not a story - it is a journey!

It is NOT a journey for the Politically Correct masses, with their 30-second clips and sidebars. It's a call to those select few who have their own dreams with visions of a better tomorrow and the courage to tell the world of doubters It's All Right to Be Different and to Be Happy with Who You Are.

Secrets

The dark cloak covering more than a half century of hidden history, has at last been torn away. Now revealed, are the countless struggles of my reluctant efforts to survive during my secret missions in the Alaskan Arctic.

As a young Veteran, I have been called upon to protect the U S national Defense System against Soviet invasion from over the North Pole, during the height of the Cold War of 1960. Mine is a traumatic journey of fear, hate and hell in search of courage, love, and salvation, through the frightening threat of Arctic Atomic War.

Since hated war has already slaughtered my father, brother, and best friend, I suffer from overwhelming fear of my own violent death, by War.

In spite of this trauma, to save all I love, I have no other choice but to become an Arctic Secret Agent, Battling Lies, Spies, and Wild Beasts to discover the secrets, hidden in my own mind, that might help Stop Global Nuclear War.

The Slaughter of War

My Slaughter by the Dark demon of war begins with my Struggle to crawl only inches at a time. my body jerks back as I feel the sting of the same barbed wire that ranchers use to hold back wild cattle, wire tearing at my blood-soaked clothes and slicing, again and again, into my still young flesh.

It is the late 1950s, I have just been hurled into this new world of global chaos. The Cold War is boiling over. As a prelude to invasion, Russian bombers are poised to fly over the North Pole, ready to attack the northern most U S Arctic national defense radar systems. This frigid hell is where a nuclear holocaust will either start or be stopped before it ever begins.

Along with countless other privates, I have been drafted into the military in preparation for this terrible War, a giant bird of prey, perched on the edge of total world annihilation. In just three months of this frigid hell, I must be trained to "kill or be killed" and will be forced to honor the dark demon god of Slaughter, WAR.

Here, at the Fort Benning Army Training Center in South Georgia, the winter is not yet over, but the torrents of early spring rain have already turned the solid earth of bricklike clay into perpetual mud. As with the other young, frightened Army grunts around me, I am forced to realize this is not a night of pretend games, for just beyond our darkening horizon looms the threat of yet another holocaust of War.

To prepare us for our role in this world of chaos, we are forced to face the screech of flying bullets and deafening concussions of exploding bombs. We have been told the bullets must be real to help us fully understand the dangers of war. There is no room for mistakes in battle, so there must be no mistakes in our training. I am afraid, yet I cannot escape this trauma all around me.

I shudder at the thunderous roar of the bombs violently exploding in foxholes, spewing out geysers of the smelly, stagnant winter rain. The pulsing sounds of machine guns vomit out their endless tracer bullets, creating a stream of Haley's Comet tails. Glowing streaks of death light up the cold, pitch black Georgia sky just inches above my head. In all this turmoil, crawling just ahead of me, covered in the same putrid mud, is my best friend, George. He is already a hero in my eyes. Turning his head, I can see George yelling, "Hey Evans, keep your butt down, or you're gonna get it shot off".

George is totally fearless, with the courage I can only imagine discovering within myself, someday. Yet, after almost three months together, I have discovered my fearless friend is afraid of one earthly creature, No mere human, but greasy, slimy Snakes. Another bomb explodes so close that I can no longer hear it. Instead, as a wild beast of War, its concussion roars deep within my bones.

After this eternity of swimming in frigid, winter mud together, my friend suddenly stops. For us, time now stands still. Of our many months of training together, the past hours, days even weeks become nothing but an instant of evil silence overcoming our world of Hell. He panics when suddenly one of his slimy enemies squirms up against him, and strikes. I know George well, I know what he will do now, what he must do. As if to force me to take part in this deadly battle for life, this demon of slimy mud, holds back my struggle to grab my friend's slippery boots. I, miss.

Before my angry eyes of failure, George instinctively jumps up to run, He looks back at me and screams his last word on earth, my name, "Wayne!" as he is violently cut in half by the relentless streams of burning machine gun bullets.

For an instant I stop breathing in total disbelief, then gather just a fragment of the great courage my friend once had just seconds before. Forcing my quivering lungs to cry for help, but with only the light of streaking bullets to pierce the darkness, we cannot be seen. My feeble voice cannot be heard over the deafening noise of exploding bombs. But my brain demands I try to get help, even though I know my friend is already dead. Even in death, George tries to protect me from the numbing cold. His warm bloody remains blanket my shivering body.

Still deaf from the concussion of exploding bombs, I vow to survive and honor the memory of my best friend, my Army buddy, "Private George," for all Eternity. I must discover the dark soul of War and learn the secrets of how to conquer it. For now, I am still alive. But what of George, For George, there is No tomorrow, No first leave to go back to his loved ones, No chance to be that officer others believed he could be, No life, No love, No children's laughter, Just a government letter of an unavoidable training accident and regret.

The Bomb's concussion is still just as real, the Bullet's pain still just as real, the Red of Blood still just as real, War, or just training for War, it is still just as real, My beloved friend, Private George, is still just as, Dead.

Yet I am still alive, With the roar of bombs echoing in my brain, this glowing stream of slaughter comes searching for its next victim, Me!

Oh GOD, How I Hate War! Damn you, Damn you to Hell.

The Real World

Two years finally pass, and with all my military awards I am honorably discharged back to civilian life. Outwardly, I continue to appear to be a very successful and stable soldier who has done his duty for his country. But because of my new secret radar and communications system training in the Army, I am taught well how to Lie and Deceive.

The real world of the late 1950s is far from average. It is one of constant Threats and Fears. Threats of another World War. The reality of my new life soon shows its ugly head. Many desperate months have passed since my release from active duty, yet meaningful employment is not mine to have. Even though all the knowledge I earned while in the Army is still of value to the military, these same talents are of little use in my new civilian world. It is now a world of unbelievable struggles.

Then, as if by a miracle from above, a letter arrives from a clandestine government agency. I am offered a position, not as a soldier, but as a well-paid secret agent on a critical mission of national defense using the same specialized military skills my civilian life has long rejected. But I have to accept this government offer within a 90-day window, before a special training session in Alaska begins then a year of total isolation.

Just before noon, on the 90th day, I report to a little-known hotel, walk down a dimly lit hall, and pause at a door with no number. Turning back is no longer possible for me.

A knock on the door, a pause of seemly hours, and then a sterile, bland voice almost whispers, "Enter."

I open the rusty-hinged door and step into a one-light-bulb room, blinds down, to squint at a plain-suited man behind a small table. The man points to a folding chair and slides a document to me. At the end is a place for three signatures, dates and strangely, even time.

The suited man asks me,

"Do you need to read it again?"

I hesitate and answer, "It makes no difference now."

"The Government will withhold all the funds you earn until your 15-month contract has been successfully completed, precisely at 12 noon, on your very last day of your agreement. Your emotional or physical hardships, even your death, will not alter this agreement. If you survive the Arctic, but fail in your mission in any way, the funds held for you will be forfeited and you must leave as you came."

The suited man then points to an X. I assume that's where I am supposed to sign my name, and I do so. Before I have a chance to write in the date, the suited man takes the document, dates it, and looks at his watch and pauses. We both sit in silence. I look at my watch. Two minutes to 12 noon. I must have arrived a little early for my meeting. More silence, then the suited man glances one more time at his watch and writes in the date and time by my name. Precisely 12 noon.

He then picks up the agreement, signs it just out of my view, and puts it in his briefcase, saying, "You'll receive further instructions," and points to the door.

As I leave for home, I wonder, Why was there a third signature line? Who will sign it, and when?

It is at this time I am finally driven to change my name. Burned in my memory is being covered in my best friends blood. His last word on earth, as he was being slaughtered was my name, WAYNE. That frightful name must be buried deep into my soul until I find redemption and freedom from the guilt of George's murder. All those I meet in my new world of uncertainty will only know me as David.

My new Life of Discovery

Silently I sit in a distant Chicago airport, nervously waiting for me to be taken on my impossible journey into the frightening Arctic world. Yes, taken to that place were even God would never want to go. A place where, if He ever chose to give the world a long-overdue flushing, that's where total human isolation would be, the Arctic. Yet I am not going to this frightening world by any demand or commandment from above, but by my own Free Will. As the plane begins to roll down the runway, I struggle not to shout for it to stop and return me to a normal life.

The rumbling of the plane's tires against the pavement pounds in my ears, then quiets, and we are at last in the air. Like it or not, this agonizing journey to the Alaskan Arctic begins.

I know not when and where I will be, thousands of miles from home. All I know right now is that for a very long time I will no longer see Chicago, with its chaotic Midway airport, its spaghetti-like expressways, and its majestic skyline, for they are dissolving into the darkening clouds of a possible Midwestern thunderstorm. I wonder if this is some kind of sign, warning the pilot to turn this plane around and make a safe landing while he still can,

I suddenly jerk awake. We climb higher and higher, until we are on top of those clouds by at least a couple of miles. I don't know how high this plane flies, but I know the up and down pressure changes make my ears clog up and then pop. Sometimes it even hurts a little, but chewing gum helps my ears clear up faster.

Even though this is a very fast four-engine airplane, the trip already seems extremely long. I have been told that these four-engine planes can fly, for a while at least, with only two engines working. I hope we don't have to find out the hard way if this is really true. Even though I am afraid of heights, I try not to worry about the engines anymore.

As we taxi to the terminal, the flight attendant tells me my luggage is being transported to my next plane. I wonder, what will my Arctic lifeline be? A big plane, small plane, or a dog sled? I climb on board my next plane, which will take me in only one direction. North.

With a strange look in her eyes, the flight attendant looks at me and asks, "Are you sure you still want to take this journey of your young life forever North?"

What a strange thing for a person with her professional training to say to a passenger. It's as if she is trying to frighten me out of taking this flight. Or am I just imagining it from the dark side of my mind?

Now, I have just been told my next plane seems to have developed an engine noise and we need to return to the Seattle airport for repairs. After a successful landing and a very long break, I'm told the plane will take longer than expected to repair. This same flight attendant tells us there is another plane, a not-as-roomy-and-quiet military planes, available. She also tells us there are two important air force bases near Anchorage, and some military personnel are on board who are expected to be there this evening.

I am also expected to be picked up at the airport tonight so that I may report for my first day of training tomorrow morning. By her anxious speech I believe her home base is also Anchorage, and after a long cross-country flight she, too, would like to get home tonight.

With no other choice, with all the other stranded passengers, I drag myself to whatever flying object will take me forever North, again and again.

A "not-as-roomy-and-quiet military aircraft" is an understatement. It has only two engines, and it is the same olive drab color as that old army uniform, I am so desperately trying to forget.

Fire, Fire

My seat belt is fastened, my barf bag is handy, my deodorant is actively fighting my sweat, and all those instructions about seat belts and emergency oxygen are completed. The plane begins to roll, and roll, and roll. Then lift off, and the rumbling noise stops, until two loud thumps (wheels coming up, I hope). Hurrah, finally up in the Wild Blue Yonder!

As my plane goes higher and higher into the air, I have no head or stomach problems, yet. Both engines on this very old Army plane seem to be purring fine (at least I think so) and all appears to be well. The seat belt light goes off and everybody unbuckles their belts. I can do the same...uh, on second thought, maybe not. But at least I do put my barf bag away.

I am really lucky to have gotten a large window seat (yeah, lucky). Getting instead up enough courage to actually look outside, I follow along the wing and expect to see the end of it disappear into the black of night. Instead, I am shocked to see, of all things, the engine is not only glowing red and white, but is actually belching fire like a medieval dragon! What about the other engine, the one I can't see?

My deodorant is now on major overload and my barf bag ready for a quick redraw. In panic mode, now, I call the flight attendant over and point out this possible little problem with, at least this engine—maybe both—being on fire. She smiles, and whispers in my ear, "That's normal, sir. Coffee, tea, or Coke?

This young lady is very calming but may be lacking a little knowledge about burning airplanes. She is also probably very attractive—but I have another very important issue on my mind just now, like survival, and why did she question me about my flying on these planes taking me forever North?

before I realize it my flight soon ends with a safe and happy landing. It's now the thump of those wheels finally coming back down, I have been a true survivor once again. Yes, a survivor, not so much in the actual physical sense, because there was no real engine fire, but in a very emotional way. I conquered some of my fears of flying, fought the battle of my mind, and I won. Or did I? I soon realize I cannot yet imagine the battles I must fight to survive in the eternity of months before me.

Arctic Training

My new home is at a secret location outside Elmendorf Air Force Base, Anchorage, Alaska. Here, I will be trained in the operation and maintenance of the top-secret radio equipment used to guard the entire coast of Alaska from Russian attack.

The schedule is grueling during the week. On weekends I am free, and even expected, to explore the far north world around me, when accompanied by my fellow students and instructor, for security reasons.

Since the information I am taught is classified, I am told not to disclose anything dealing with the project to others.

The special radio communication systems I was trained to use in the military are very similar to what I am now being taught. This is very helpful during training, but later causes me to wonder if being first in the class is always the best.

One of the greatest honors I have during this time of training is meeting and talking with one of the most honored inventors of the 20th Century.

In his younger days, he was the assistant to the man who invented television. He became the inventor of the system that saved so many lives and helped defeat the enemy during World War Two, radar.

He also invented the same technology that I learned and was taught in the military, microwave radio. He is visiting our training center on an inspection tour because it is those same technologies of radar and high-power microwave that are used to transmit the radio signals from site to site within the Alaska National Defense system.

After reviewing the background of all the students, he asks to speak with the person with the most experience and knowledge of some of the equipment he helped invent. The school director introduces him to me.

As we talk, he describes in detail the inner workings of this transmitter tube he named a "Klystron." I believe his only regret might be the extra heat and dangerous microwave radiation they generate, which requires a liquid cooling system and a shielded cabinet. He says he believes people will someday cook with this same microwave radio energy, but with far less power and danger than the transmitters I must use.

For many reasons, I will forever remember our talk together, especially the details about the heat and radiation problems, and I am inspired by his passion and want to be an inventor like him. The world lost a great and caring man just weeks after we spoke at the training center. His name? Doctor Russell Varian.

The special radio communication systems I was trained to use in the military are very similar to what I am now being taught. This is very helpful during training, but later causes me to wonder if being first in the class is always the best.

With my three months of training completed, it was time for our site assignments. Instead of the best site, Anchorage I felt I earned, I am assigned to the communications site that's most critical to protect. It's also the coldest, darkest, most dangerous, and most isolated location in Alaska, the northern beach of the Arctic Ocean. It's the first point of any enemy invasion from Russia over the North Pole. It is so secret, isolated, and dangerous that civilians, especially wives, are not allowed.

At first, I am very disappointed. Then, I realize I was picked because there was a need to have the most technically experienced persons at this most critical site. I figure I should be proud of that and accept the mission to go to the Arctic, vowing to do the best job I can.

The next night is a traditional going away party with my fellow training friends, The following morning begins the most fearful journey of my still young life as I board my first small bush plane.

The journey is pretty straightforward. I'm in a decent plane with at least a couple of engines and some kind of heater. Where am I going? North, forever North to the Arctic.

Nome Tour

The first part of my journey is relatively quick. I see we are approaching a town that doesn't look anything like a small town in my area of Hammond, Indiana. We approach the runway. The plane sets down fairly quickly, then we roll off to the side and stop. Hopping out of the plane and greeting the pilot I met when we first got on, I ask, "How long do you think we're going to be here?"

"Oh, probably a couple of hours. We have to unload some merchandise and then pick up some skins and things from the Eskimos here. Why don't you take a little tour? There's plenty of time and you may meet some interesting people."

After a short walk I reach what must be the main part of Nome, just a small town. There are all kinds of attached buildings with their doors open, as it is August and still fairly warm. I walk into one that's much like any small country store in Georgia, Alabama, or Tennessee. The small stove in the middle of the room is old enough for Ben Franklin to have built it himself.

As I look around, I see an elderly woman, and I walk up to her. "It's a very interesting little store you have here. May I look around and maybe take a little tour around Nome?" I ask politely. "I'm on the flight going up to the next level, Kotzebue, and then I guess I'm going to go up further north to a place called The Cape."

"Do you mind if I walk around town? Is there anybody who could show me around?"

"Oh, yes, my husband. His name is Nanook."

"Where is he?"

The next thing I know I hear this sort of deep, masculine powerful voice saying, "Right behind you."

"Whoa, where did you come from? I didn't hear you."

"I'm just a quiet one when I walk. You have to be quiet around here when you're sneaking up on Polar Bears, Caribou, and other wild animals."

That really disturbs me, but I don't want to show it.

"Of course, I understand, Nanook. But hopefully, I won't be running into them and have to sneak up behind a Polar Bear or Caribou." I remember a Caribou is sort of like a big burly second cousin to a reindeer, but a lot meaner.

Nanook is a very friendly Grandfather type Eskimo. During our tour, I learn a great deal about the strange history of Nome.

Time is getting late, we head back to Nanooks country store. With friendly farewells, and a short walk, I'm back at the Nome airport. But where is that shiny new plane that brought me here? Instead, In see parked on the runway, is something that looks like the Wright brothers may have experimented with it in the early 1920s.

My pilot tells me, "We had a little engine problem with the plane you came to Nome on, so we had to borrow one from a local bush pilot. He says he has had it since it was new and that he keeps it running himself, so it's perfectly safe to fly. He'll do the flying."

I nervously ask my first pilot, "Do I have any other choice?"

He smiles again, knowing I have no other choice, and tells me, "Your new bush pilot really knows his way around up here. He usually takes tourists hunting Polar Bears to his favorite sites and has only lost a few who wandered off. He'll get you to wherever you are going just fine."

Bottoms Up

Once on board, I find this new plane does not have the comforting security of the earlier purr of four engines, or even the two of my military plane three months ago. Instead, I am boarding an ancient three-engine monster with a new, much older, bush pilot—he's at least 45 or 50.

I am so dead tired about now; I really don't care what engines might already be dead or what they sound like as long as this thing has wings. I will even take a giant albatross, or eagle, or whatever they have in the Arctic that won't eat me and will just get me where I am supposed to go.

With the takeoff roar of this strange airplane's engines now more of a gentle hum I start to doze off. In this, the even colder wonderland of the Arctic, and in my groggy daze, I say to myself, Well, at least it isn't that Dog Sled, yet. Time for a little snooze, maybe a big one. But I'm a little bothered by the strange feeling I have about my new Arctic friend Nanook back in Nome. His wisdom appears far greater than I would have ever expected from an aging fisherman and shop owner.

I wish I could spend more time with him as my mentor learning the hidden secrets of the Arctic. Maybe we might talk again some time, some place, at least when I stop at Nome on my way back a year from now.

I think I am dreaming when the roar of at least one engine, maybe even all three, jerks me awake. It is not the comforting, soothing hum of those many powerful engines that have become part of my travels and provided me some reasonable Arctic comfort. Instead, I begin to hear and even feel the deafening roar of only two engines if I'm really lucky. Why is there all this coughing and sputtering? What form of air travel is this? If I get to wherever I'm going, what am I going to live in? Will I have a one- or two-story igloo? What strange creatures will try to room with me?

I soon realize that the roar of the engines is quieter now because one of them, the center one, has a propeller that isn't turning anymore. I look over at our, hopefully, extremely experienced bush pilot, but he appears to be totally unconcerned with our plight.

I can only believe that this engine's quitting is nothing new to him and has probably happened quite often in its half-century of existence. Maybe it's just like our aging pilot, taking a nap in midflight.

With only two engines left, after many miles on this unbelievable journey, one starts to sputter again, and a winter storm is quickly developing. The pilot tries to call for help, but the signals from his aging radio are too weak to reach their destination.

He must search for the Kotzebue village beach with his eyes alone, using dead reckoning and his memories of the flat, soggy tundra he has traveled many times before. With only one good engine and the plane losing altitude and sinking lower and lower, the pilot gets the sputtering engine to run enough to finally reach the beach of Kotzebue. After a safe landing, supplies loaded and some temporary repairs, the pilot believes he has fixed the second engine.

First, there are fresh fruits and vegetables. At least I won't have to worry about dying from sailor's scurvy. Then, I notice some very smelly live chickens. Oh, what I'd give for an aspirin right about now.

With countless hours later, I wake up and believe I am sitting on the tip of the nose of a White Polar Bear, perched on the edge of the Arctic Ocean. This nose is actually the tip of a mile-high mountain that looks just like a very large, life-threatening Polar Bear Head, when seen from 8,000 feet. It's the home of a top-secret government radar site staffed by 150 air force "volunteers" and a few insane civilians, like me. I realize, of course, it could be bombed by our enemy at any moment.

We are approaching some kind of a small runway, I think. I hope. As we barely pass a one-story building acting as some shield against the wind, he is swerving our plane side to side, up and down. Or is it Mother Nature reminding us of who's really flying this plane? Not us anymore.

We are violently thrown sideways and headed for the Arctic Ocean. Our pilot struggles for enough control to swerve us back toward a very short beach. Another gust of wind tilts one wing toward the frozen sand. Our only remaining engine struggles to right us, but I can see we are not going to land gracefully on our wheels.

A wing tip, an engine, and a wheel all bite into the solid sand at once.

With a sudden, back-breaking jerk, we are upside down with the frigid Arctic waters lapping at our heads.

All the crates are tearing away from the cabin walls. My luggage and my freed chicken friends are violently propelled towards me now. All I can do is raise my shaking hands across my face and pray. Then, with a sledgehammer of pain crashing into my brain, Black Arctic night descends upon my conscious mind and my world of reality disappears.

My First Day

Wow, that night went past too fast. Just, where am I? Oh, yes, in the Arctic. Yes, in the Arctic now. For a very, very long time. Jerking awake, it's my first lucid day in Mother Nature's ice box. A quick shower, some clean and less smelly clothes, and then finally dressed with a smile plastered on my face. Just how long was I out, hours, or maybe even days. Someone is knocking on my door. It's time to go, but go where and how do I get there? I finally meet Eddie. Each day this new friend has looked in on me, from the moment I first crashed on the beach.

Eddie introduces himself as my driver to the radio site on top of the mountain. An expert mechanic, Eddie explains his specialty is operating and maintaining the Arctic snow vehicles, especially the two he calls Weasels. Because of Eddie's apparently caring nature, I hope that over our next year together I can develop a friendship with Eddie.

In a huge, strange-looking truck, we leave our base site, a place we have not even seen in full daylight yet. We struggle to climb a very narrow road blasted out of the side of a mountain that must be at least a million years old. This very first trip up is not a gentle tour on some yellow brick road. It looks very narrow for even just one truck to pass,

"What is that thing coming to greet us around the corner?" It looks very angry.

Eddie tells me it is a buck Caribou. The Caribou is thumping on the dirt road, apparently trying to decide how much of a threat we are in this very large, crazy-looking truck. I think that if this very large, equally crazy-looking animal really tried, he could knock this truck— and both of us along with it—right off this mountain, where we are almost 4,000 feet up, give or take a few hundred feet. So, who is counting right now? Not me!

This beast suddenly stops his pounding on the road. Thank goodness, it looks like he doesn't want to battle us after all, at least not today. I partially open my right-side truck door, swing my camera over the top edge and snap a picture of my very first animal in the Arctic wild. Suddenly, Eddie yells a lot of four-letter words at me over the deafening noise of our truck. At the same time, he yanks me back into the truck, slamming and locking the door behind me. He then hollers something about it not being a south forty-eight state family petting zoo up here.

Starting to thank Eddie for his quick action, I am interrupted by the sight and sounds of our not-so-tame buck Caribou walking, then running as fast as a speeding bullet. Eddie hollers something about bracing ourselves for a full-frontal impact.

Here he comes, thundering straight at us, so very close that I think I can actually smell his breath and see myself reflected in his wild, angry, glassy eyes. Here comes the big hit, but instead, he abruptly swerves his half-ton body towards the side of the truck. My side!

I feel the massive rush of air coming at me, like being in front of a speeding train just before it flattens me into just another railroad tie. The air pressure coming from this giant beast painfully pushes against my eardrums, or is it the thunder of his hoofs pounding our only escape road into fine dust?

His horns dig into my door, with the chilling screech of nails on a chalkboard. Our giant of a truck begins to rock sideways and skid even closer to the edge of our very narrow road. I am waiting for the end of my life that has just begun, and I never even got my first paycheck yet.

The screeching from horns raking my metal door finally stops. Eddie and I quickly turn our heads backwards the best we can, without leaving the safety of our Sherman tank. Our not-so-friendly Caribou is finally past us.

He slowly trots to the side of the road. He gradually works his way down the mountain. I believe he is probably gloating about his victory over these invaders into his land.

With our most immediate danger over for now, Eddie tells me "Well, you got to remember this has been their land for a very long time. We're the strangers in town up here. You have to be prepared to protect yourself from about anything big, and even bigger. That's why you carry that 44 Magnum on your hip."

How desolate the perfectly flat landscape ahead looks compared to the constant mountain we have been traveling. Traversing those last few twists and turns just before finally reaching our buildings looks dangerous enough to maneuver on a semi-sunny day like today. I can just imagine how treacherous these same curves will be to manage in the dead of winter, soon to come. Finally, we are on the very top of this-mile-high mountain.

I get out of the truck to take a better look at this monster of a vehicle that must have come from another planet. It looks a lot different than it did in the dawn's early light thousands of feet below. Just what is all that extra equipment installed on it used for, anyway? I guess I will find out sooner or later,

My new Arctic office

I soon see my new workplace up close. It has a very large radar dome and an equally large number of strange-looking radio antennas; some may even be seven stories tall. I am warned that if I stand too close these superpower microwave systems can damage, or even fry, a lot of my body parts.

Over my shoulder I see Eddie coming towards me from the main building. You'll meet your partner, Lee, on the hill tomorrow Let's take a tour, since we still have light for a long time. A walk will help us get to know each other, Dave.

Our isolated Arctic home

Off the narrow dirt road and finally at the bottom of the mountain, Eddie shows me this big pool of water. "What's that for, Eddie?" "That's our freshwater that comes from the melting snow as it trickles down underneath the permafrost.

Eddie then points at the buildings that will be our home away from home for a long time to come.

"Hey, Dave, did you notice the little trap doors across the roofs on the buildings when you flew over them coming in? Well, just pray that we don't have the kind of snow I guess they get around here once in a while. It gets so deep that it buries the dumb building, and the crew has to come and dig us out."

" We'll just slow down a little and talk about what's going to happen over the next year to both of us. Why do we work up here? Why are you here?"

Eddie says, "Well, you'll find out that we have a number of fellas working different shifts because we have to keep the communications and radar place running twenty-four hours a day, seven days a week, or the bad boys will attack us.

Since we're the closest ones to them, they will get us first. There is a saying up here 'The first to know and the first to go' if a War ever starts. That's us, Dave.

"They're going to target us, knock us out and take over from here, then go on down the Alaskan coast, taking the rest of our Arctic brothers out. That's why we're pretty important up here, to stop them. Don't go thinking you're just another one of the regular people up here. Oh, no. We're up here for a reason, and it may be that we have to really do the thing we got to do. That is, we may be the ones getting our comeuppance up here, if it turns out that we really get into a War. Yeah, that's why we have three work shifts, because we have to make sure that somebody's fresh on duty. I don't think you ever want to be caught up there by yourself. Sometimes it takes a couple of people to fix all that technical stuff, and you're one of them.

"We have generators for electricity, and these generators keep the heaters in the big antennas to going to melt off the ice and snow. The also keep your old fanny warm in that big communications building up there. It's the same for the guys in the radar dome and down here, but you can't waste electricity on any cooling machines. That's where mother nature comes in to help us.

You see, were sitting on the side of a mountain that's made of ice at least a million years old. When this place was built, they blasted a hole in the side of the mountain right behind all the buildings. That became our frozen food locker. We just simply built the storage building right into that. That's where Cookie makes his great meals. You'll meet him later. He keeps all of the food and everything that can spoil in his big Mother Nature freezer."

Eddie tells me the next day I finally meet Lee and begin my training on the actual communication equipment on top of this mile-high mountain I'd soon learn to call "The Top." I am supposed to be an expert in keeping all this fancy electronics stuff alive. Sure. All that book learning and lab work back at the Anchorage training school for three months is one thing, but now I have been thrown into the "fix it or maybe die" national defense world.

I soon have just a month of added equipment training that keeps me very busy, and I learn our mission on the Cape well. But now it's September, which means the beginning of real Arctic snow.

Food Locker Destruction

"One evening as we descend to the base camp, Eddie shouts, Hey, Dave, let's go get some vittles. It's lunch time." Cookie has always been able to rustle up some mighty fine vittles, as Eddie would say.

Upon entering the lunchroom, some of the others see us and shout, "Hey, Evans, did you hear what happened to all that food we got off the barge last month, which is supposed to last us until the end of next year? Well, it ain't."

In the middle of all this confused chatter the base captain enters with a call to attention. He then breaks the bad news to us.

"Enough of all this scuttlebutt. I'm here to tell you the straight scoop. As you all know, there is no need to have an electric freezer to store our food up here, when we have a mountain made of million-year-old ice right behind us. "

For years that big hole blasted out of the ice right behind Cookie's cooking area has worked great to keep everything as fresh as we can. But no longer. Just after our yearly food supplies got off the barge and were stored there, safe from all the bears, and ready for our delicious meals...no moaning, guys, about Cookie's fine cooking...there was a not-so-slight accident.

One of the older bulldozers stored on the hill began to leak oil. It ran between the still-frozen permafrost layer and upper tundra soil, finding its way into our mountain-side food locker. The leak was so slow that nobody noticed it until now.

A great deal of our food was ruined. Most of the good stuff off the barge didn't make it, and Cookie had to toss it. As you know the Arctic Ocean is starting to freeze over pretty much now. So, that's it for any more barge help.

The food we got off the barge last month, which is supposed to last us until the end of next year? Well, it is not. No beef, ham, or turkey. It's going to be a pretty lousy Thanksgiving and Christmas without it. Now, as much as you hate messing with Mother Nature up here where we are only visitors, we need some kind of meat and protein, or we'll all get pretty sick soon. I need some volunteers to hunt down some of our Caribou neighbors and lug them back here, after saying a prayer of thanks over their souls, "I must warn you, if you accidently run into an entire herd, this could turn into a very dangerous mission. Anybody stepping forward?"

I hear one courageous person jump up and say, "I WILL!" "Eddie, you're volunteering?" I jump up and holler, "Me too!"

Eddie and I round up all the Arctic clothing and survival gear we can carry. Maybe too much, when I realize, somebody will have to lug back hundreds of pounds of literally dead meat. I wonder who?

Alone for Eternity

I now have learned enough about all this complicated communications equipment to repair a few things, if needed, but there is so much more to know, so much to understand. I feel I can handle most uncertainties ahead of me if given enough time and added training.

I am so thankful to have my fellow worker, friend, and mentor beside me, Lee. He is a soft-spoken, mature, much "older" man, of at least 35. He is a great instructor, both thorough and very patient.

As we prepare a small lunch together, Lee tells me he is not feeling very well. Probably too much of that smelly Caribou meat. I find some stomach medicine in our emergency aid cabinet. He takes some of it but says he's still in pain. I think we've had enough of this self-help doctoring, so I call down to the base camp and declare a medical emergency.

A medic tells me the weather report does not look good,

33

with a winter storm coming, but he will send up their best driver. I know old, reliable Eddie is the one picked to rescue Lee. Since we always have two operating personnel on our site for every shift for safety and for emergency situations such as this, I know I will be with the very best fellow operator coming up with Eddie to replace Lee. I hope he is someone who can teach me new repair tricks like Lee always does.

I try to make Lee as comfortable as I can while waiting for Eddie and our relief person. Minutes seem like hours as Lee's condition worsens. Even with all the howling wind, I finally hear the noisy tracks of our snow vehicle, packing down mounds of rapidly falling snow. Everyone calls this rumbling miniature tank, left over from World War Two, a Weasel. I really don't care what it's called right now as long as it gets Lee back home to medical help.

I open the main door only a crack, and the increasingly violent wind rips it out of my hand, sucking much of the heat out of the building. Through the never-ending black of Arctic winter sky, I can imagine this strange Arctic storm is rapidly becoming a frigid Arctic tornado, forming directly over the radar dome.

Even in this driving snow, I can see Eddie hunched low, almost crawling face down, battling to reach me, but I don't see anyone else. Working together, with all our brute strength against the ever-growing wind, we finally are able to get Lee to the Weasel.

Eddie works his way to the other side, gets in, and slams his door against the driving wind. The rumbling engine still running from his trip up, Eddie turns the clanking machine around as I nervously wave goodbye to them both. I turn to see the last of our giant antenna disappear into a white world of nothingness and hope it will still exist tomorrow.

Our courageous Eddie came up for Lee but brought nobody else to take his place. I can only imagine the challenges against this storm they must have down at the base just to keep our home in one piece. They probably need every able-bodied man, too. Maybe they all think I am pretty good at running this place, which is okay by me most of the time. But, with an Arctic winter storm from Hell like this coming, I'm not so sure I can keep this vital electronic communication station up and running alone.

However, I know I must keep the radio system working no matter what. I perform my list of duties, checking everything over. Once again, Alone

I realize it has been many hours of waiting and that the weather is getting even worse. I check the doors and windows. All secure but weakening. Since the power cables are buried deep in the mountainside, I will have life-giving warmth and light as long as the generators far below at base camp stay alive.

So it is, too, with the buried telephone and teletype cables from the radar dome 1,000 yards away, between my own communication building and the base camp. There is only one place where these critical wires rise out of the ground to be connected together—in a small, isolated closet, out of sight and out of mind.

With the equipment shaking, even greater wind speeds, and lower temperatures, I begin to put on the first of many layers of Arctic clothing. Not much later, still waiting for added help to come for my relief, I begin to realize that even with Eddie's expertise of traveling in ice, snow, and wind, relief from below is beyond reality.

With Hurricane Winds and extreme cold, the radio communication systems begin to fail. Conditions getting worse, I finally understand my disintegrating communication site is for me to keep alive... Alone!!!!!

The Russians Are Listening

In the meantime, in the Bering Strait, off Alaska's coast, on a strange-looking fishing trawler, two young Russians are spying on my communication site by monitoring my ever-weakening radio signals to Kotzebue.

"Alexis, Alexis!!! Their radio signal is almost gone. What does it mean? Why is it happening?"

"We have to be absolutely certain this is a serious matter. We cannot report this to Moscow and have it turn out to be a false alarm. A lot of terrible things could happen to us if we are wrong".

Silence

On my dying mountain, the constant chatter between the radar dome operators (just 100 yards away) and the support team at the base camp far below is gone. All calls of enemy danger from the mile-high mountaintop to the outside world become nothing but deafening silence.

It is then I realize I am not really alone. Doctor Varian my inventor friend from the Anchorage training center comes to mind. Repeating the doctor's warning about his Klystron transmitter tubes' temperature problem. "If they get too hot, they will burn up. If they get too cold, they will stop working altogether. That's why there is a special cooling system for them."

I realize that with the room's temperature already at freezing, the cooling fluid still pumping around the critical transmitter tubes may soon freeze and cause the tubes to die. But, if I turn off the pump, thus stopping the cooling fluid, the tubes may stay just warm enough to transmit some small level of radio signals. That way, somebody further south will realize I am still alive, and that the transmitter building has not been blown of the mountain into the Arctic Ocean—Yet. with no way to call for help, and nobody to ask for guidance I must, once again, make the terrible decision...alone. I must disobey all government rules I have vowed to honor. If it works in keeping some radio signal alive and I survive, I may be honored as a hero. If it fails and the tubes are destroyed, my reckless action may brand me a saboteur and traitor. Gritting my chattering teeth, I turn the pump off.

NORAD Screams

Meanwhile, deep inside an isolated desert mountain in Colorado, it is near chaos at the United States North

American Defense Command Center known as NORAD. Here, the National Emergency Alert system goes off with deafening screams.

"Captain, get that damn noise turned off! It's probably just another of the thousands of tests we have had to live through since this stupid cave was first built years ago. While you're at it, find out what the hell is going on. Just to be safe, seal the center. Nobody enters. Nobody leaves."

"Yes, General." Well?"

"It's a real alert, General."

"Where?"

"Alaska, sir."

"Well, Captain, that's a mighty big place. Can you be just a little more specific?"

"It is our White Alice Coastal Radar warning system protecting the upper west coast, facing Siberia."

"How bad?"

"We have lost all communication above the Kotzebue Air Force Base radar site."

"So, you're telling me, Captain, for the first time ever, our early warning communication system facing those damn Russians has a busted link?"

"Yes, General."

"Where is it?"

"The Cape."

"Isn't that the uppermost site, right on the Arctic Ocean?"

"Yes, General."

"Do we know why it has crashed?"

"Our weather people guess it's probably due to a major Arctic storm."

"How bad?"

"The last known communications from there reported one-hundred-fifty mile-an-hour winds with a real temperature of 90 below zero."

"Those poor souls. They may all be blown off the mountain and frozen to death by now. How long have they been down?"

"Almost a day, General."

"So, Captain, with our super intelligence system, we are just now hearing about it? With the damn Russians just a stone's throw across the Bering Sea from the Cape, their spies probably know more about what's going on up there than we do!"

"Maybe, General."

"There is no maybe about it. We don't know what kind of a spy operation they have up there, but maybe this mess-up will be just the thing to cause them to slip up and we can flush them out."

"General, that would be a major breakthrough for our intelligence team."

"Yeah, and we may only wind up sacrificing over a hundred of our best people up there to get this information. That's a pretty lousy trade off, Captain."

"How long has our system been down, and us blind to Russian intentions? How long would it take for them to take some serious action against us?

"I'd give them three days before that tickle up their butt

about our site failure turns into a full-blown gas pain and they would explode in our direction."

"Well put, Captain. That tickle is called invasion, son. Finally, the 'Big One' that nobody in their right mind would ever want to start."

"Where would they come from, sir?"

"Over the top, Captain, and Santa couldn't stop them. What's the weather report at the North Pole?"

"Our best information, without the Cape's radar, is just about clear."

"Oh, even if our guys are still alive, they are socked in by that damn storm and couldn't even see what hit them. I know this super-secret communication equipment isn't worth a damn right now, but can't we call them on a plain, old stupid telephone?"

"No, sir. Phone poles and wires can't be installed in the Arctic ice. That's why we put in that long-range radio system."

"Once again, 'for the lack of a nail'...never mind. You're too young to know what I am talking about. Well, we don't have much of a choice but to pray those people up there are still alive and are smart enough to repair the damage when the storm is finally over.

I even hope the Russians really are spying on us some way and know when we are back up with our radar watching every move they make again. It's frightening to even think how less than three days could make or break us, and maybe even the whole damn world."

"General, they were all handpicked to go up to this site

because of their superior technical knowledge and ability to work under pressure."

"Well, Captain, if they don't get their butts in gear pretty soon, they will really know what pressure is, especially when fighting off the Russians. Who is the most experienced person up there who can take over and make things happen fast? Look him up."

"The top student in the latest Anchorage training class, with a great deal of additional communications knowledge is named Evans."

"I sure hope he is as good as he thinks he is, with the guts to stay alive and lead the others to find the mental and physical limits they need to create a miracle, for all of us."

Radiation Death

In my disintegrating mountain refuge, the last life blood of human warmth is being sucked out of me, as the wind whistles through every widening crack and crevice, creating the screams of 1,000 bats. Even shreds of my undershirt jammed deep into my ears cannot keep the growing deafness away.

The shattered glass of small observation windows becomes arrow-sharp shrapnel hurled into my thick but fragile parka. The comforting glow of the electric lights, once powered by giant buried cables and massive generators, flicker in a dance with death.

After what feels like an eternity of freezing and struggling to keep some semblance of life in my failing communication system, and myself. I collapse on a table and am forced to be next to the only source of warmth I have left, the lethal-powered radio transmitter. Its protective doors have been torn open by the violent shaking of the building.

The dying, but still powerful, giant transmitter tubes spew forth deadly radiation. The same lethal forces of human annihilation unknowingly leashed upon humankind by the first Atomic Bombs used to end World War Two.

Should I miraculously survive my battle with Nature, this radiation is destined to destroy my seed of life and so condemn my children never to be born.

Freezing Death

Dreaming, I believe I have died as a failure and a coward on the mountain and left all those I love behind. Yet, from the darkening world of freezing death, I feel the ever-growing warmth of spiritual light growing within my very soul. Then, from a distant mist begins to appear the shape of a friend I think I know, Nanook, or is it the spirit of someone or something that has come to answer my dying prayers.

The Miracle Begins

Nanook begins to instruct me in the understanding and uses of his Subconscious mind. Nanook will tell me what he will learn is knowledge from Nanooks ancestors coming from Tibet hundreds of years before. This is not true, for David could not believe or comprehend the fact that these are mystical powers I already possesses that Nanook will help me discover from deep within his subconscious mind.

I open the door of my mind finding the secrets of the mysteries of the Third Eye and with it his visions of his Future; Mind/Body Control; Out of Body travel; Self Hypnoses; and the ability to recall facts, faces and places from the photos I have taken while on my Arctic journeys. From this I learn the art of Photographic Memory. Nanook then discloses ways to survive the frigid Arctic cold by sleeping buried under the snow, next to resting Husky dogs, I learn the truth behind the proper building of an ice and snowstorm shelter, the igloo.

In just a few moments of my unconscious true world time, Nanook says he must go back to his home. His time with me is complete, he departs into the mist and golden light from which he came, he leaves a fatherly parting message in my reborn subconscious mind and the truth behind of his Arctic visions.

"You have become a faithful student and friend. With your Arctic Miracle of your third eye in which to see your own future, teach others that they too can achieve their own miracles with hope and faith in themselves to conquer any darkness in their heart and see a brighter tomorrow.

"A job well done, my son, a job well done".

Through the darkness of my own death, the light of rebirth, With the help of my spiritual friend, Nanuck, Arctic miracles are born from my very soul and the power to use my third eye to see the future of my mission to help others is clear.

Rebirth Miracles

No longer in a dream state, I force my eyes open to see if the world still exists. I am alive again, and the screaming bats and violent shaking are deathly silent. Although badly damaged, the walls and roof of my communication building still exist. Even as dark and cold as I know it still is outside, I feel a growing warmth in my body and soul. and can even see a brighter future for me and my loved ones. It's truly an Arctic Miracle.

Still barely holding onto my small shaking table by the open transmitter doors, I hear a telephone ringing, or do I? I really can't hear sounds very well. My ears are still stuffed with pieces of my underwear. They were not much noise protection against all that screeching that came from every crack and crevice in this groaning, swaying building.

The more I become aware of my surroundings, the more I realize the building no longer feels as if it's being torn from its crumbling foundation.

Almost three days and nights I was without sleep. Still in a daze, I feel this storm of the century must be subsiding, at least to some degree. The wind has dropped from 150 miles per hour at 95 below zero to a gentle 60 miles per hour, a mere breeze compared to its former self, though I don't think "breeze" is the right word yet.

I see the needles on our four receivers starting to rise just a tiny amount off zero. The dense, stormy sky must be thinning a little and letting our weak radio signal sneak through to the

Kotzebue site over 300 miles away. I don't know yet if it is really a phone ringing or my wishful imagination. I take the pieces of my underwear out of my ears, probably very dirty and smelly after 3 days in this Arctic Hell.

I look down the main hall at a floodlight pointing my way. Some great scientist attached it to our phone line so it would flash when a call is coming in. As much as my groggy, frozen brain allows me, I strain to hear that friendly ring again, but I do not. My body groans with every move after days of freezing temperatures, and my blood is now as thick as Jell-O.

I must force myself to get off this table of death and do my best to close these radiation protection doors before my rescue arrives if they are even still alive down at the base.

What words of wisdom can I dig out of my still-confused mind?

"Wire."

Now mentally and physically strong enough to fully rouse myself, I am finally able to move and speak.

How can anything be wrong with the wires? They are all buried in this mountain, except for where they come out of the ground into the wire closet. Wire closet?

"Once all the phone and Teletype wires were attached, there was no reason for me or anyone else to go back in there. I don't even remember where that closet is. After all, there is nothing in there but stupid telephone wires. Telephone wires?

Still groggy, I struggle to walk through the halls. I

eventually find the wire closet at the very end of an isolated hallway. Opening the door, I feel a blast of frigid Arctic wind. The small observation window has been shattered by the storm. The wire rack is covered with drifts of still-blowing snow.

I have no shovel to remove it, so I scoop out the snow with my hands. Then, I discover the wire mounting rack has nearly been torn off the wall. All the solid copper wires were sheared off their electrical terminals by the wind's violent shaking.

In the dimly lit room, I take off my gloves to feel where to reattach the wires. I barely connect some that appear to be the most important, but they instantly break, as the mounting rack is still shaking from the wind streaming through the open window. I make several attempts to salvage the wires, but they break every time. I know then that they are too short from all the breaking, and too brittle from the numbing cold, to be repaired any further. The wires are too cold, too short, and too brittle. I realize flexible wire will move with the wind and can be stretched. But where am I going to find such wire?

I slam the door shut against the still-howling wind. Still weak and half crawling, I search every room. All of the main lighting is fluorescent bars, but I find tiny lamps in the lounge area. Ripping the wires out by hand, I make my way back to the wire room. I open the door, only to find the wind has caused the snow to drift back over the wire terminals.

Once again, I search through accumulating snow to uncover the hanging wire rack and search for the correct broken telephone wires. Even in my half-frozen, delirious mind, I know that to safeguard the nation against enemy attack I have to repair this most critical link. It is the heart of the communication system between the radar dome and the base camp below.

The room is almost pitch black, so I have to force my bare, numb hands to work from memory. Having no wire strippers, I use my teeth to tear off the insulation. With the precious few pieces of lamp cord, I patch the critical wires. I then scoop the constantly drifting snow away from the door and close it securely against the howling wind. Still not believing in such simple miracles, but too weak to doubt it I turn around and open the closet door one more time, praying to see the dangling, lifesaving lamp cords still alive and working

To my amazement and joy, our miracle lamp wires are still attached, in spite of all the remaining twisting and turning caused by Mother Nature's wrath.

A Savior's Rescue

Exhausted, I stumble slowly down the hall to our phone, my one hope for rescue. I anxiously await the next lifesaving ring. As I sit there my brain awakens a little more and it finally dawns on me not to just wait for a call from below to me, but to call down to them. Hopefully, my friends are still alive in that warm, quiet oasis I called home so many days, maybe even weeks, ago. Actual time is lost to me right now.

Before I can make that critical call down below, the phone rings. I know when angels call upon us, we may hear the sound of their beautiful harps. Since it's not harps, I hear, I finally believe I'm not really dead yet. It may not be harps, but this ringing sound from Mr. Bell's invention is just as beautiful to me, right about now.

Out of the corner of my eye, I see that marvelous beacon of light flashing, just for me, so I know this call of survival must be real. Just in case the phone is much colder than I would like, I quickly grab a rag on the floor and put the receiver close to, but not on, my ear.

Not being able to say any words in days, not even to myself, I force my voice to say that magic word of greeting, "Hello?"

It's Eddie. He says, or is it shouting, into my still dull ears? "David, are you alive?" I realize this true friend cares for my health and know he doesn't realize how dumb his question is. I cannot say "hello" if I am dead. His deep concern for me on my first day, and again now, I will never forget.

After I assure him, I am actually alive, he tells me things have been bad down below during the storm, but he knows not as terrible as it must be high up here in the very eye of the storm. He knows that being on top of the mountain, I did not have the side of this giant mountain as a windbreaker to protect me as they did down below.

He now shouts very loudly, probably thinking that even if the phone lines fail, I could still hear him. He says he is coming for me with the Weasel, which has had some problems, but he thinks can make it. He also tells me that he is bringing up not one, but two, relief people. One is a repair technician who will try to resurrect a few more phone and Teletype connections and fix the window. The other is someone who insists on coming to my aid, even though he is still a little ill.

I know my constant savior, Eddie, must be bringing back my site supervisor and good friend, Lee. I hope he is well again. I tell Eddie to have the technician bring up a lot more lamp wire and to remember to turn the transmitter's cooling pump back on.

Eddie warns me not to get too anxious about waiting. He is not sure how long it will take since the snow and drifts are very deep across our fragile mountain road.

The NORAD Miracle

NORAD is still in its perpetual "wait and see" routine, preparing for the final Global Nuclear War that all pray will never come.

"General, it's over. The miracle you asked for finally came. The Cape site is back up and communicating with us, and our radar boys have eyes on the Russians again. They undoubtedly know it, too."

"Great news, Captain, but remember our orders. This loss of our national defense site, the Cape, never happened. We have all been told to wipe it from our memories. If it ever leaks out, it's a court martial, even accusations of treason for all of us, and you know what that means. What is the name again of that young man up there, who is probably the one we have most to thank for our miracle?"

"Evans. Yes, General, we certainly do have a great deal to thank him for. He undoubtedly saved so much more than just our lives."

"General, it's a pity that because of all the secrecy, the world will never know of what he did for us and can never give him a proper 'Thank You.'"

Collapse

After my three-day ordeal, Eddie is finally successful at getting me down to the base camp. For days I collapse into a state of near-death unconsciousness trying to recover from extreme cold and near starvation. Dreaming, I believe I died as a failure and a coward on the mountain and left all those I love behind. Through the darkness of my own death, the light of rebirth, the Arctic miracles are born from my very soul.

Spiritual Friendship

As his final act of friendship and love, Nanook visits me, now down off the mountain and in a deep recovery sleep. Here, he whispers in my ear.

"A job well done, My friend, a job well done".

With his loving family of dogs and sleigh he disappears

into the winter flurries and heavenly light from which he first came.

Killer Stairs

For days I collapse into a state of near-death unconsciousness trying to recover from extreme cold and near starvation.

I finally jerk awake and holler "HELP! HELP!"

Eddie, who has been perched on a chair outside my door since rescuing me from the mountain, rushes to my side. "What can I help you with?"

Still in a daze, I say, "No, not me, the young man outside the hallway door has fallen down the stairs outside and is freezing to death."

"No, that's just you remembering your terrible three-day storm."

I strain to whisper, "Go see."

Eddie believes I am hallucinating and hesitates to leave me alone. But, after covering me again with a blanket, Eddie does as I ask as I collapse back to sleep. The next day I finally wake up, but feel very weak, dehydrated, and hungry. Eddie hears me stirring and opens the door. I am sitting on the edge of the bed, still bent over from weakness.

Becoming more conscious of my surroundings I ask, "Is that you, Eddie?"

I struggle to remember the phone call on the mountain, when Eddie asked, "Are you alive?" but I can remember nothing about my rescue. I only remember the worst possible storm, the cold, and the pending destruction of his communications building.

"How long was I out?"

"Four days," Eddie replies.

"Where have you been?"

"Sitting outside your room in a lounge chair."

"I am hungrier than a Polar Bear. Did you get anything to eat out there?"

Cookie kept bringing me something and never let up on telling me to go back to my room and get some sleep. All I said was no way, no how until he is fully awake. He needs me."

I ask about the frozen man.

"He is being flown to Kotzebue for treatment,"

Eddie says. "How did you know about him falling?"

"I heard him calling for help."

Puzzled, Eddie says, "That's impossible. This place is like a World War Two bunker and the door outside to the stairs is at the other end of the hall."

I shrug, "Well, that may be, but I didn't just hear him; I felt him freezing to death,

"Eddie, tell me about the storm down here."

"You know, an Arctic storm comes and then goes just as fast. We mostly got nothing from the storm here, but we knew it might have blown you away, especially when we didn't hear from you for days.

You know, you threw me for a loop on that lamp cord you

told us to bring when we came up to get you. I knew that was a pretty fast trick you pulled to get us talking together and the radar boys telling us again what might be going on with those Russians."

"How much new snow since then?" I ask.

"None."

Eddie's Shock

"Well, Eddie, do me a big favor, as crazy as it sounds. Go around the building and look outside my window and tell me if something strange is out there."

Okay, you asked for it, Dave."

Eddie returns shortly and knocks on the door as he enters. "No such thing," he says in bewilderment.

"Well?"

I look at Eddie and grin.

First mumbling, and then a little louder, "I looked for Snow sled tracks in the snow", I found just a few. The tracks just barely sank into the snow, kind of like there wasn't even a person sitting on it. but that ain't all, the craziest darned thing is that there were no dog tracks at all."

"What the heck is going on?" Eddie asks, me somewhat angry.

With another grin, I told him, "You wouldn't believe me if I told you."

Battling Walrus

After surviving a death-defying time in the Arctic, on a day off, I'm taking a Sunday stroll along a desolate beach. I'm trying to relax and remember that I will be going home soon.

All of a sudden, I can not only hear a great commotion. With my now Arctic miracle, I now see my immediate future. I can't believe my eyes. I spot two walruses fighting in the distance. this future will not be a happy one if I interfere, so I crouch low and duck behind a small hill. The walrus is a beautiful animal, but a ferocious fighter when sparse Arctic food or a prized mate is at stake. Soon the growling and cries of the battle are over, the wounded loser leaving behind a broken and bloody tusk.

Carefully picking it up, many thoughts go through my mind. I feel sorry for the Walrus that lost his bloody battle but, at the same time, his broken tusk is a wonderful souvenir that I can keep forever, never forgetting the many adventures—both good and bad—I have experienced, and how lucky I am to be going home soon.

Polar Bear Lunch

My friend Eddie calls to tell me he needs a part delivered to him. He is up on the mountain having trouble with the Weasel. The problem is that the only truck available to go up the mountain has a little problem of overheating.

Eddie tells me just to wait it out until the engine cools and then continue on. So, aware of the problem, I start up the mountain and, sure enough, there is engine trouble.

After waiting for a while to let the engine cool off, I have trouble starting it. Knowing that Eddie is expecting me, I need to let him know I will be delayed. A life survival shack, with the only telephone, buried deep in the protective Arctic ice, is not far away.

I have been told in my Arctic training that life shacks were placed along this narrow road in case anyone has trouble getting up the mountain. It is supplied with food and warmth necessary to survive until help arrives. Approaching the shack, normally surrounded by complete silence, terrifying growling noises penetrate my ears. Getting a little closer I see big footprints in the snow.

Immediately grabbing my camera, which I always have with me, and still being a fearlessly crazy young man, I take a picture of these giant footprints.

I see my future will not be a good one if I interfere with my not so friendly polar bear having lunch. I had better get back to the truck, as the roaring is getting louder. No more investigations for me today. I realize I dropped my keys in my rush to get back to the protection of the truck. I start to panic, retracing my steps and looking for them. Going back towards that survival shack and checking into those giant footprints is not an option. No, not in my pockets. What a relief to see a tip of shiny metal in the snow just outside the truck door.

With my newfound miracle, I look for my battle to come. I don't see the Polar Bear, but he is still cussing a lot. He must be too busy trying to find a can opener to think about having me for lunch, and not as his guest. The truck starts and I am on my way again. You know, if that beast had shown up, you can be sure I would have taken his picture. After all, a person doesn't join a Polar Bear for lunch every day with himself on the menu as the main course. The roaring finally stops. Gunning the engine, I muster enough nerve to look behind me where there are more angry polar bear tracks trailing away from me. Thank GOD for miracles, especially for my own personal one of being able to see visions off my own future before another possible violent death.

Eddie's Last Mission

Months later, with many other adventures behind me I have successfully completed my year of duty and earned all the funds for my dreams to come true.

Eddie has also served about a year and is scheduled to leave just one day after me. "Yeah, you get to fly the coop today, and I'm stuck with one more job. The boss wants me to take my Weasel to the mountaintop site for some early winter testing.

You could call it my last impossible mission. Hey, that's got a nice ring to it. Maybe someday, since you've been the brainy guy around here, you can write some exciting stories about all the crap we have been through together.

After sharing more stories of their times of danger and joy together, Eddie tells David, "Well, enough of this sob stuff".

56

Waving one last time, he shuts the door. Then, Eddie opens the door again, just a crack—the last time he would ever do so—and whispers, "To be eternally free of your guilt and fears, you must discover the courage you have always had, and you will find the truth, the reason for your existence. Believe in yourself, and those who watch over you and believe in you. The truth will set you free."

I am speechless. Over the past year together, I have never heard my good friend, of a plain and humble background, speak such words of wisdom.

Day 455- The End

My bags are packed, and before my flight Cookie escorts me to the dining room for one last meal on the Cape.

As they enter the dining room, the captain calls, "Attention!"

The entire room stands up, raises their glasses and shouts, "To the man who stopped a Nuclear War!" Then everyone applauds while I stand there looking bewildered.

Cookie explains, "By monitoring the Russians' radio traffic, talking about your weakening signal problems during that three-day storm, our counter-intelligence group discovered the Russians gave up any idea of a first-strike invasion onto your site.

They backed off because you plugged any possible holes in our Alaska National Defense Communication System by keeping your signal alive, in spite of your three days alone and freezing. Your sacrifice of three days in frozen hell turned the world away from the death of hated War towards the seeds of lasting peace.

"Enough," says the Captain. "Those terrible days are over for all of us. We are still alive. No invasion."

Cookie then takes a strangely familiar piece of paper out of his pocket. He signs it with the date and time, just as the dining room clock strikes exactly 12 noon. All of my friends applaud again for a job well done. Exactly to the very minute, my 15 lonely months—455 days on my Arctic mission are finally ended.

Cookie tells me, "You have earned every penny, and more, for doing your job for the past year in this hell hole. In fact, on your way back, stop by our government headquarters in Anchorage and pick up your bonus, a very sizable bonus. Oh, by the way, they want you to take charge of the construction of a completely new Alaskan national defense radar system starting immediately. Of course, you would be away from home again for over a year. Think about it–very hard–but not too long."

I then realize Cookie is much more than "just" a cook.

Homeward Bound, Maybe Not

The joy of my last meal with friends for the past year is interrupted by an announcement that the first winter storm is starting to blow in from the Arctic Ocean. I know from experience just how unexpected and unpredictable the first storm of the winter season can be. These storms may start moderate, but then explode into Arctic Hurricanes. The snow always begins on the top of the mountain and works its way down, which is why Eddie was chosen to go up there to check out the new snow tracks on the Weasel.

The loudspeaker announces my plane for home has taken off from Kotzebue village on schedule. I pray the storm is not so bad that the pilot would have to abort his attempt to reach the Cape.

Cookie tells me, "You know, this early in the winter season it happens all the time. These Arctic bush pilots can fly in anything. Even tundra mush soup. As he gets closer, he'll be calling in any minute for landing instructions. It will work out just fine. Come on. Let's eat. It's your favorite food, Caribou."

Upon hearing this, I almost gag. "The only food I had to eat during those three days of nightmares alone on the mountain during that winter hurricane was frozen Caribou meat. For breakfast, lunch, and dinner. After the first day, I could eat no more. I believed, with one hundred fifty miles-an-hour winds at ninety-five below zero, I would certainly freeze to death long before I starved."

Realizing my emotional reaction to his not-so funny joke, Cookie apologizes, "Only kidding, Sorry," and brings my real last meal on the Cape. "It looks and smells great, Cookie."

Love or Friendship

There is no time to eat. The captain of the base reenters and calls, "Attention!"

This time, he is not greeted with happiness and cheers. He announces an explosion and fire have just occurred on the mountaintop.

"Who's hurt?" I ask, my voice cracking as I tell myself I probably already know.

"Eddie," is the captain's single reply, his eyes downcast.

I jump up shouting, "I must go for him!"

The captain says, "Evans, I know he has become a good friend, but your year here is up today. Your plane to take you back home may be landing any minute now. I have two others going back with you who also deserve to go home, so I can't hold up the plane until you get back down."

The Captain continues, "Eddie's many other friends are desperately searching for ways to rescue him in this storm. Eddie is doing what he loves with his crazy Weasel. He is doing what he feels is his duty. Your duty, while here in the Arctic, was to help save your country in times of War. It's over for you. Go home to your loved ones, now. That's an order.

"Sorry, Captain, I know you want to help me. I respect you, but I don't need to follow your orders anymore. As you just said, my tour is over."

The Captain pleads, "With the Arctic weather changing so fast, Evans, it may be days, possibly weeks, before another plane can make it back for you. You can't miss this one."

Terrible Decision

"You're right, Captain, but in spite of the storm, I'm going up top to get my friend Eddie first. He needs me right now.

Rushing to the motor pool, I see Eddie's fellow mechanic and friend, Bob. "Where's the other Weasel?" I demand. "It's down for repairs."

Normally known as Mr. Cool, I feel desperate to help Eddie. My physical being feels every instant of Eddie's final struggle to survive. The roar of the other motor vehicles' engines being tested and tuned up for winter is not helping my mood at all.

"Ok Bob, What bucket of bolts do you have that at least runs and is gassed up?"

"Just the boom truck, but it doesn't have any tire chains on yet, and may be a sliding death trap up there without them in this freezing snow."

My mind can no longer bear mirroring Eddie's suffering. I must put my dream of a new life behind me for now. I command my total self, my mind, body, and soul to go try to save my friend.

Again, Bob warns me of the ever-growing storm and danger on the icy mountaintop, but I remember what was taught by the greatest teacher of self-sacrifice over 2,000 years ago, There is no greater love than to give one's life for a friend. "Forget the lousy chains. For Eddie, I'll take the damn truck!!!"

Rescuing Eddie

Without even seeing the radio site, a vision of the truth flashes in my mind—the violent explosion and flames engulfing Eddie's Weasel, the noxious fumes of leaking gasoline, the screams from Eddie's scorched throat, and the agonizing pain of Eddie's soul crying for deliverance. I gun the truck engine and barrel up the narrow mountain road to Eddie.

I know I will have to drive across the ice against strong crosswinds to reach Eddie, but since the boom truck has no tire chains for gripping, I could be blown off the mountain to my own death.

The closer I get to the top, the stronger the wind blows, blowing the truck sideways across the narrow mountain road. I try to drive crosswise against the wind, as in a sailboat. Whenever I stop, the tires stop sliding. When I try to move slowly forward, the tires slip and the truck slides again. I am stuck.

Determined I will reach my friend, I rev up the engine, completely flooring the gas pedal. The wheels spin but cause enough friction to burn through the thin layer of ice under them. It is just enough of a break in the ice for me to gain traction.

I finally reach the top. In an attempt to stop the truck, I try to turn it broadside to the ever-growing wind, which causes me to slide even more. The wind pushes the huge truck across the ice, right into the side of the communication building, sealing the access door needed to remove Eddie. On a stretcher, Eddie will not fit through the small observation windows, the only other way out.

I shout to the two men on duty, "Climb out and help me

push this damn truck away from the door!"

After clearing the door, I realize Eddie cannot sit up in the passenger seat, but the truck's storage area is loaded with maintenance equipment. The stretcher won't fit, and the equipment is too heavy to carry into the building to make room for Eddie.

Over the howling wind, I shout, "Just push all this junk out of the truck onto the ice ground and slide it out of the way!"

As carefully as possible, I and Eddie's other friends put the stretcher with Eddie in the truck and force the doors shut against the battling wind. I then begin the treacherous journey to get Eddie to medical attention at the base camp below.

As difficult and dangerous as it was to drive up the sloping ice, going downhill will be far worse. The downward slope is a twisting snake of ever-slippery ice. The growing Arctic wind could force us to the very edges of the narrow road and plunge us thousands of feet below to our deaths.

Charging Beasts

I'm about to turn the last icy corner to what should have been a safer road, one protected from the storm by the height of the mountain. Instead of a safe, snow-free path to the base camp and Eddie's medical aid I can see just around the corner, that I will be greeted by three giant Caribou charging towards us, blocking the narrow road of our only escape. I believe the one in the middle is the same glassy-eyed beast I had met on my first day at the Cape, now back to even up the score. This time he brought his whole smelly gang with him.

As I hear my friend, Nanook, told me "You cannot eliminate fear, but you can control it. Remember that the Hook, muffler, horn, and buck are your tools of fear. Turn them around so your enemies fear you more than you fear them".

I have always called this strange truck a monster. Now I have to turn it into a giant one so fearful as to stop the inevitable Caribou stampede.

Die? "No! Not in this Frozen Hell. No! Not after all the crap I have been through".

I gun the engine with the roar of the missing muffler, I lower and violently swing the hoisting hook, blast the bullhorn, and buck the monstrous beast back and forth. Now primed to attack, I gun the engine again and pop the clutch, sending clouds of dust and early winter snow into the heavens.

I fix my gaze on the glassy eyes of that giant Caribou I met that first day and I turn my unbelievable fear toward my Arctic enemies. Uncertain as to what monster is attacking them, they stop their charge. They turn around and race to get out of my way, fearing to be pushed off the mountain.

I then see over 20 more Caribou coming up the narrow road behind the first three. Gunning the engine even more, I take on the entire herd in battle, three Caribou at a time. They, too, run from my monster from Arctic Hell.

With the road finally clear of wild beasts, I race Eddie to the medics. They tell me they will take care of Eddie, and for me to get on the plane that has just landed after being delayed by the storm.

Heading Home

I rush to the airstrip, where I see a "true" airplane with two beautiful, shiny engines ready to restart. It is not the bucket of bolts that almost took my life as it crashed on the Cape beach so many lonely months ago. My baggage is already on board, loaded by the other two agents who are waving me on, as they are anxious to get home.

I am deeply worried about Eddie who, for a solid year, became not just a friend, but my second-best friend. Even a brother.

I look back one last time at the base camp. The days of almost 24-hour of pitch black, frigid winter are giving way to the days of almost 24 hours of sun light. I realize I will not see it ever again. After a solid year in isolation here, thousands of miles from modern civilization, my airplane of deliverance begins to roar with the mighty power of those two magnificent engines. Unlike the one-engine bucket of bolts that limped its way onto the beach runway so many long months ago, this angel of heavenly flight is still right side up. The plane begins its smooth roll and then lifts me effortlessly towards a heaven of long-forgotten happiness. The pilot loops back over the Arctic Ocean and slowly passes the dining room windows.

This time, not to shield us from the treacherous Arctic winds, but to let us wave one last farewell to our friends who wish they were with us, on their way back home. Gaining altitude, our trusty pilot makes one more pass over our little shacks tied together with the fragile threads of companionship, so desperately needed in this land of perpetual loneliness. Off in the distance is the narrow road to the mountain that holds the memories of so many exciting adventures that threatened my very survival.

A restless nap, and soon Nome is on the horizon. Then, the landing approach and the smooth, almost silent touchdown. After we coast to a stop, I ask the pilot if I have time to visit some old friends in town.

He answers, "Sure. We will be here about two hours.

As I stroll towards the center of Nome. I am shocked to no longer see the simple store with the wooden walkway in front. Finding a wandering Eskimo, I ask what happened to my friend Nanook and his generous wife? He sadly responds that they passed away just a few months before.

After an almost a silent thank you, I struggle to leave my fond memories of my Nome friends behind. Soon I return the airport to begin my next journey towards my almost forgotten life of yesterday.

Anchorage, Money, Memories, Regrets

Our landing at the Anchorage airport is soft, almost silent, and even relaxing after a full day of my never-ending journey south, far away from my life in the Arctic. I'm scheduled to fly to my next stop, Seattle, the next morning, so I might as well use the extra daylight to my advantage. With my overnight bag in hand, I rent a car. As Cookie told me to do, I first stop at the headquarters of the hush-hush government group that hired me so many months age. There I find no gate, no guards, only the collapsing training buildings with the musty smell of dying memories.

Spies, Spies, and More Spies

Back at the company office I walk in, greeted by the manager. "Welcome back to the real, Wayne. That's how we made out the cashier's check for all the great work you did at the Cape and for completing your mission. No More Spies for you. You're quite a celebrity to many up there, especially Cookie. As he told you, we also have a sizable bonus check for you. You have certainly earned it as our reports on the enemy's Bering Sea activity shows with the Russians."

"I have something extra for you. It's not much for all your valuable accomplishments in Alaska, especially at the Cape. It may be just a piece of paper to most, but when you display it on a wall in your new home, think of it as a unique medal your grateful country has awarded you, a special son, in which it is extremely proud."

Certificate of Appreciation

Wayne W. Evans
This testimonial is awarded for having faithfully, loyally, and
ably performed his assignment as Station Technician on the
White Alice Communications System within the Boundaries
of Alaska on a project Vital to the Defense of North America.
In witness whereof we have here to set our hand and seal This
6th day of August 1960
Federal Electric Corporation
Operation and Maintenance Contractors to the United States
Air Force for the White Alice Communications System.

"Sir. This is quite an honor. Thank you. How is the new National Defense Radar and Communications System coming along?"

"You know I can't tell you that now, but I can tell you it won't be long before you won't need to worry about 'spilling the beans' concerning all the technology you learned about and protected up here, because it will soon be obsolete."

"So, it is okay if I put this nice Certificate of Appreciation on a wall back home?"

"Certainly. It just says, Station Technician. But you can even tell your family what you really were up here. 'An Arctic Secret Agent Battling Lies, Spies, and Wild Beasts,' as you put it, but don't be surprised if nobody believes you. Thank you for all your hard work in protecting our country.

"Let me shake your hand again for a job well done, Wayne,

and don't lose those checks.

"Yes, sir."

He then salutes me. I salute him back, for the last time.

Reborn

After an anxious and restless night and the sun slowly rising, my plane of deliverance begins to roll. I have only dying memories of my year in the Arctic. My travels of thousands of miles of forever North will soon end, a journey that began so many months—or was it years— ago... Alone. Now, though, my life's journey is played in reverse. My camera is no longer hanging around my neck waiting for that next exciting shot. No more attacking Caribou. No more photos with the snowcapped mountains of Alaska off in the distance. No more islands, or tiny villages and ships along the coast of Canada. These are images of my past that will soon be replaced with those of the new life waiting for me just over the horizon.

Yet, I still have other images of many hours and thousands of miles back at the Cape. My new subconscious powers can feel that the medics who examined Eddie knew that there was no rush for me to bring him down from the mountain. He was already dead from the explosion. They left Eddie in the examination room to go get his records. When they returned, Eddie was gone. There was no trace of his body and there were no records of him in their files. It's as if Eddie had never existed!

Clearing my mind, I realize I have a long way yet to go to finally be back home, reborn and with all those I love, once again.

Thank GOD and maybe his angel, Nanook, for my own personal Arctic Miracle. At last, with my third eye, I am able to see my future so I may fulfill my destiny to help others find their own life of meaning.

Some Closing Thoughts:

"Laugh with Vigor,
Love with Passion,
Dream with Courage."
W. D. Evans

"This is Not the End.
This is Not Even
the Beginning of the End.
It May Not Even Be the
End of the Beginning."
Sr. Winston Churchill

"Life is not measured by
the number of breaths we take,
but by the number of moments
that take our breath away."
Unknown

Searching For The Good War

Arctic Friends

Slaughter of War

Last Dance

Parting Kiss

Darkening Tomorrow

49th State

Mighty Bears

Almost There

W D Evans

No, he is Not "The Most Interesting Man In The World, from TV commercials, and "Indiana Jones" from Action/Adventure movies, But he is Very Close: Arctic Explorer, Secret Agent, Decorated Soldier, Academic Scholar, Honored Inventor, Recognized Artist, Unique Musician, Respected Teacher, Successful Gambler, Firm Entrepreneur, Surviving Pilot, Versatile Actor, Prolific Author, Proven Lover.

With over 60 years of exciting adventures together, Wayne lives with his lovely wife, Annie, in Milton, Georgia, just outside of Atlanta. Through many difficult times, they are proud of their professional and family accomplishments together and of their four children and seven grandchildren.

The foundation of his own multiple accomplishments is his loving family. Wayne's philosophy is to live each day to the fullest by helping his Children, Grandchildren, and others yet unknown. As a 6 book Author and an inspirational Speaker, he instills in others the belief "It's Never Too Late to Make Your Dream Come True".

At 86, he is a true Renaissance Man with a long life of surviving death, so is now known as

"The Man With More Lives Than a Cat".

H M Logue

I am proud to be a wife, mother, grandmother, and friend to many. When I met Wayne at the local airport, my husband, Richard, was a flight instructor helping him overcome his fear of heights.

I thought" what a nice man". I had no idea we would become fast friends, nor did I have any idea of his achievements, and brilliance.

I had a passion for reading and Wayne was an inspiring writer. Wayne loved to write about all his many life's adventures, six books so far!

Wayne often gave story telling speaking engagements which Richard and I would attend. After we reviewed several of his books together, Wayne believed I possess significant understanding of literary structure. This was probably because of my passion for reading.

Much to my surprise, he asked me to co-author his next book. I had no earlier experience in proofreading and editing but was delighted to give it a try. What a responsibility and privilege!

I thank you Wayne and your wife Annie for being our friends and expanding our lives in endless magical directions.

My Arctic Miracle

David Goliath
and
The Man with The Third Eye.
(Coming Soon)

What if You had the ability to see the future, oh not everyone's, just yours?

Is it a blessing, a path to Enlightenment or a journey into the Dark Hell of despair? It would be the ultimate test of your God given Free Will to choose the right or wrong path, even good or evil. Each decision you would make could change the world for the better or might destroy all you love, forever.

My Name is David Goliath
Am I real, or just an aging writer's imaginary Alter-Ego?

As with the first David from the distant past who slayed the giant of Hate and Fear, I am forced to take the name of Goliath. It is my forever reminder of my constant battle with the dark side of my being, while searching to find the hope and light of a better tomorrow to pass onto others.

Another True-Life Adventure Series
From
The Man With More Lives Than a Cat™
W D Evans -author
wevansee@gmail.com – 770 753 4181

"Angel Annie" and "David Goliath"

"Life is not measured by the number of breaths we take, but by the number of moments that take your breath away."

"It's Never Too Late to make Your dreams Come True."

David Goliath and the Arctic Miracle.
Is there Life After Death?

Through the darkness of my own death, and the light of rebirth, can I discover mystical powers to see my future that will not only alter my own destiny but also that of the entire world?

This is not a story - it is a journey!

Along my life's path of more than 85 years I have experienced over 24 life-threatening events that I desperately try to forget, but then realize they are agonizing tests of my will to live and go on. This is its message to live each day of loneliness with hope for a better tomorrow, have faith in yourself and a greater power, believe in all those you care for and those who care for you.

From the team of
W D Evans and H M Logue.

A short story based upon the True-Life adventure novel.

"Searching For The Good War".

by W D Evans.

The Man With More Lives Than a Cat

"It's never too late to make your Dreams come true"